מסורה

ArtScroll Youth Series®

Rabbi Nosson Scherman / Rabbi Meir Zlotowitz
General Editors

Tales To

Parables based on Pirkei Avos

Published by

Mesorah Publications, ltd

LiveBy

written and illustrated by master storyteller and artist

Rabbi Yitzy Erps

Table of Contents

The New Watch 5

Painting With Pride 9

Prince Albert 15

The Broken Light Switch 21

A Mouse on the Loose 26

New Tefillin 32

A Night to Remember 37

Zutchka 43

The Parking Space 48

Who Is Truly Rich 52

What's the Big Deal? 57

ARTSCROLL SERIES®

TALES TO LIVE BY

© Copyright 2009 by Mesorah Publications, Ltd.
First edition — First impression: May, 2009

Published by **MESORAH PUBLICATIONS, LTD.**
4401 Second Avenue / Brooklyn, NY 11232 / (718) 921-9000 / www.artscroll.com / comments@artscroll.com
Printed in Canada
Custom bound by Sefercraft, Inc. / 4401 Second Avenue / Brooklyn, NY 11232

ISBN-10: 1-4226-0900-6 / ISBN-13: 978-1-4226-0900-2

The New Watch

"Excuse me, sonny. How would you like to buy a nice, brand-new watch?" Joe Shvindler asked. He had set up his sales tent at the street fair and was looking for customers.

"Sure, why not?" Sruly said. "I could use a new watch. That's why I came here in the first place. Please show me what kinds of watches you have."

"Very well. Let me see now. How about this one over here? It matches your shoes. This one here matches the tie you're not wearing today. Or, how about this one? It lights up in different colors while you're sleeping. Oh, wait a moment; I have the perfect watch for you. I know you'll love it. It can even tell time …." Joe Shvindler continued to ramble on and on, as he showed Sruly various watches.

"The one that can tell time sounds like a good watch," Sruly commented. "How well does it work? Does it come with a guarantee?"

"Of course it works well!" Joe Shvindler assured. "Did you actually think that I would sell you a watch that doesn't work? And, of course, each and every one my watches is guaranteed by the manufacturer."

"In that case, may I please have the manufacturer's name and phone number?" Sruly requested. "I'd like to call them and verify their guarantee."

"Um … sure, of course … the manufacturer's name is … um … the name is … er …. I'm sorry, the name just slipped my mind for a moment," Joe Shvindler tried to stall. "The manufacturer's name and phone number are engraved on the back of the watch in very, very tiny fine print. When you get home you can take a look with a strong magnifying glass. In the meanwhile, why don't you just buy the watch and if it breaks, we'll worry about it then."

"Er … no, thanks," Sruly said. "I think I will just move on to the next vendor."

"Excuse me young man," Mordy Tzeitler called out from the next booth. "Perhaps I can interest you in buying a new watch?"

"Yes, but before you show me any watches, I want to know about their guarantee," Sruly demanded.

"It will be my pleasure," Mordy Tzeitler declared. "We, at Emes Watches, stand by every watch we make and sell. Our name is clearly etched into the back of each watch, along with our address and phone number. We are a sixth-generation watch manufacturing company, family-owned and operated for all that time. Our watches are the most accurate and finest watches on the market today.

"If you would like, I can provide you with a list of satisfied customers, along with a copy of our company's history — from its founding to the present."

"Thank you," Sruly replied. "I would like that very much. It looks like I've found the right place to buy my new watch.

"Did you know, sir, that your company's guarantee reminds me of how lucky we Jews are. We also have a guarantee. It's our Torah that was passed down to us through an unbroken chain of genuine Sages. This unbroken chain can be traced all the way back to the time when Hashem gave us the Torah at Mount Sinai. The first Mishnah in *Pirkei Avos* testifies to this. It says: Moshe received the Torah [from Hashem] at Mount Sinai, and [Moshe] transmitted it to Yehoshua. He transmitted [it] to the elders, and the elders transmitted it to the Prophets, and the Prophets transmitted it to the Men of the Great Assembly ...."*

Pirkei Avos 1:1.

Painting With Pride

"*I* just don't get it, Dave," Gabby complained. "I've been a professional house painter for over twenty years. I used to get a lot of work, and now I hardly get any jobs at all. It just doesn't make any sense!"

"What do you mean?" Dave asked.

"Dave, take a look at yourself," Gabby continued. "You've been paint-

ing houses for only ten years, and yet you have more customers than I do. Not only that, but many of my old customers are now using you instead of hiring me again. Hardly anyone recommends me anymore. What's wrong with me? Do you think that I'm getting too old for this kind of work?"

"You're not too old, Gabby," Dave reassured.

Gabby whined, "Then what *is* my problem?"

"Perhaps it's the way you do your work," Dave hinted gently. "Maybe you don't paint with the same enthusiasm as you used to."

"Oh, really?" Gabby asked, taken aback. "What do you mean by that?"

"Well, let's compare how you do your painting jobs and how I do mine," Dave suggested.

"Okay. Let's compare," Gabby said in agreement.

"How do you start a job?" Dave began. "Do you put down drop cloths to protect the floors from paint splatters? Are you careful to cover up every piece of furniture?"

"What for?" Gabby asked. "All that covering up is a waste of time. Over the years I've developed experience. I'm very careful not to splatter. If I'm in the mood, or if the customer insists, sometimes I spread a few drop cloths here and there."

"Are you able to vouch that all your jobs are splatter-free?"

"Um … er … no, not exactly," Gabby mumbled in an almost inaudible voice.

"Do you double-check to see if you missed any spots? Would you touch up a spot on the ceiling that stands out now against the freshly painted walls, even though you were not hired to paint the ceiling?"

"Um … er … no," Gabby stammered.

"How well do you clean up after you're done?" David continued as gently as he could.

"Well, let's see now," Gabby hemmed and hawed. "Whenever I put down drop cloths, I always shake them out on the floor before I put them away. Then I gather up all my extra paint and supplies. My customers don't pay me enough to do maid service, so I leave the vacuuming and sweeping for them to do. It's good exercise for them."

"Okay, now it's my turn to tell you what I do on my painting jobs," Dave humbly began. "I always take time to cover up all the floors and furniture with drop cloths. I make sure to move all furniture out of the way, too. After I finish painting, I examine the job to make sure I didn't skip any spots.

"I'll touch up a spot on the ceiling if it became more noticeable against the freshly painted walls. To me it doesn't matter if I was hired to paint the ceiling or not. I take great pride in every job I do. I do a job with the same care as if I was painting my own home. Oh, yeah, there's one more thing I do. When I finish a job, I do a very thorough cleanup, and even sweep the floors and take out the trash, like the used tape and the dust that I created."

"I can't believe you do all that," Gabby criticized. "You work so hard for so little money."

"Actually, it's not quite like that," Dave explained. "Because I love doing a job well, I never approach it as though it's an act of forced labor. I take great pride in making sure that each job comes out great. As a result, many people give me a little extra when they pay me. And it goes without saying, the more satisfied customers I have, the more new referrals I get, and the more repeat customers I have."

"You know, I never thought of it that way," Gabby conceded. "I guess, over the years, I eventually lost my pride in doing a good job. I ended up caring only about the money. Maybe, if I start putting the same love and care into my work as you do, I will start getting better results, as I used to do."

"You certainly will," David reassured him with a smile. "As a matter of fact, you can

learn this lesson from what Antigonus says in *Pirkei Avos*. Antigonus says, 'Don't be like servants who serve their master on the condition of receiving a reward; instead, be like servants who serve their master not on the condition of receiving a reward. And let the fear of Heaven be upon you.'*

"This means that one should do mitzvos out of love, and the fear of Hashem should be upon you to prevent yourself from becoming careless."

"Does that mean that one should do mitzvos out of love and forget about receiving reward?" Gabby inquired.

"Oh, no! Heaven forbid! It means that when one does a mitzvah out of love, rather than for the sake of the reward, the reward is much greater! This concept can be applied to anything you do. People will always appreciate any work that is done out of love and care."

Gabby absorbed Dave's lesson. As Gabby's ways changed more and more for the better, more and more customers began hiring him again to paint their homes.

Pirkei Avos 1:3.

Prince Albert

"Tatty, what should I do?" Tamar cried. "I brought a ball to school today so we could all play together. But instead of playing nicely, everybody got angry at me and didn't want to play with me."

"Tamar," Mr. Trachtman wondered, "are you sure you are telling me the whole story?"

"Well, maybe there is one part I left out," Tamar admitted. "Since I was the one who brought the ball, I thought that I should be able to pick the best players to be on my team."

"Ah hah!" Mr. Trachtman exclaimed with a smile. "Tamar, I think you need to sit down and listen to this little story. It will help you with what happened today at school ...."

※—◈—※

"Did you summon me, Father?" young Prince Albert asked.

"Yes, as a matter of fact, I did," King Arnold affirmed. "My dear son, I'm sure that you realize that you will become the king one day. You are now old enough to go out and study the subjects in my kingdom. Your goal should be to develop a plan that will encourage the people to be

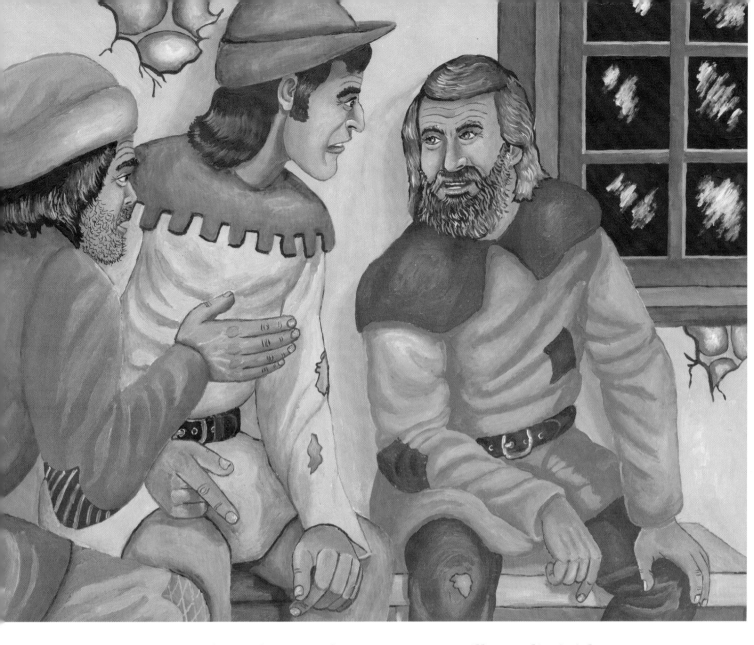

happy with you as king, but, at the same time, will not diminish your royal dignity."

Prince Albert chose to go out into the kingdom disguised as a peasant. He mingled with the local peasants and before you knew it, the prince and the peasants were deep in an interesting discussion.

"You know, Charlie," Henry said. "I'm getting tired of seeing all the rich people living such good, luxurious lives, while we peasants work so hard and are so poor."

"You're so right, Henry," agreed Charlie. "I have an idea. Maybe we should take the wealth from the rich and give it to the poor. That would balance out things. And we would become heroes to the poor!"

"But enemies to the rich," Prince Albert pointed out. "What do you gain by making the poor happy while making the rich unhappy? You'll still have unhappy citizens! Don't you think that since the rich were able to make so much money, they have earned the right to live so well?"

"I guess you're right," Henry conceded. "But wouldn't it be great if they shared all their money with us?"

"Yeah, that's a good idea!" Charlie piped in. "After all, it's not our fault that we're poor."

"Wait there just a moment, fellas," Prince Albert voiced another objection. "If the rich share all their money, then they eventually won't have enough for themselves. Rich people need to live a wealthy, respectable lifestyle. Otherwise, no one will not want to do business with them, because the businessmen will think that if they look poor, they are probably not good at business."

"Okay, smart aleck," a frustrated Henry sighed. "What kind of solution do *you* have that will make *everyone* happy?"

"I think the rich should set up funds to help the poor," Prince Albert suggested, "but the donations they give to charity should not prevent the rich from being able to keep up a comfortable and respectable lifestyle. If people followed my advice, then the rich and the poor would *both* be happy, because *everyone* would benefit.

"We all know that the king tries to help out all his subjects, within reason. Imagine if he gave away all his royal riches and lived like a pauper. Would anyone respect the king? How would he support an army to defend his kingdom? How would he pay the police or garbage collectors? Do you get my point?"

"You are so right," Charlie and Henry agreed. "You know, with your wisdom, *you* should become king someday."

"Perhaps, I will," Prince Albert said with a smile as he began to walk away.

"Oh, by the way," Charlie called out after him. " You never told us your name!"

"Oh, I'm sorry. My name is — Prince Albert."

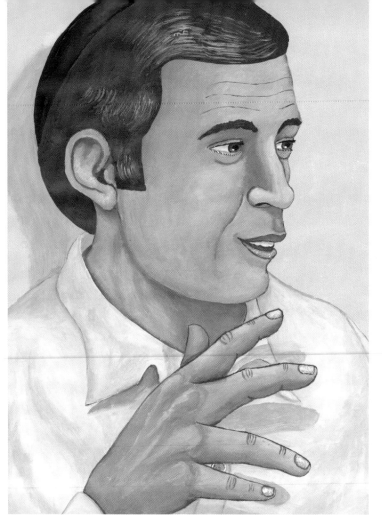

"So you see, Tamar, having the ball and demanding that you always get your way would make you the only one to be happy. On the other hand, if you would act as Prince Albert suggested ..."

"... I would share the ball and choose up fair teams," Tamar continued his sentence. "That way, I will have fun *with* the others. My classmates will appreciate me for being kind enough to share my ball — making *everyone* happy!"

"Including Hashem," Mr. Trachtman was quick to add. "Remember what the mishnah in *Pirkei Avos* says: Which is the proper path a person should choose for himself? Anything that is good for himself and causes others to admire him."*

"I guess I know what I'm doing tomorrow with my ball," Tamar concluded happily.

Pirkei Avos 2:1.

The Broken Light Switch

B UZZZZ!

"Who's there?" Mr. Finster asked.

"It's Shalom Lichtman, the electrician. You called me to fix a problem that you're having with your lights."

"Ah, yes; please come in," Mr. Finster said as he opened the door and led the electrician into the dining room. "Here's where the problem is. I can't seem to get the lights to go on."

"Did you check the circuit breaker?" Shalom asked.

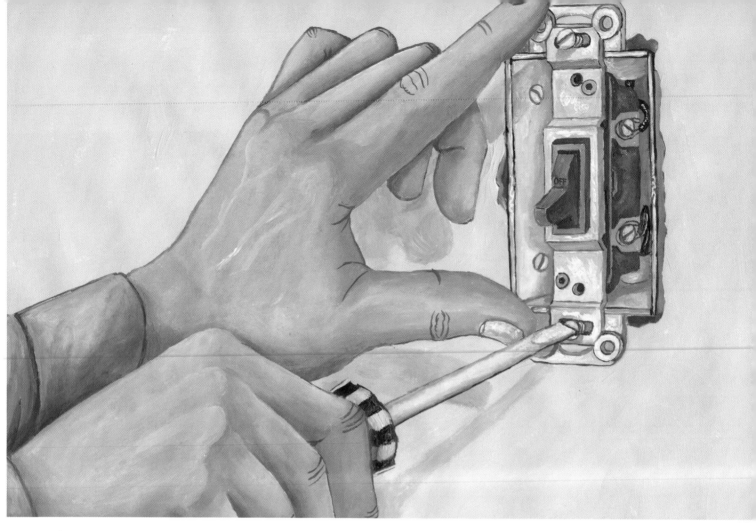

"Yes, I did."

"Did you check the light bulbs?"

"Yes. All the bulbs are brand-new."

"Well, in that case, it looks like I better check out the light switch," Shalom suggested. "It's possible that the wires inside the switch, which are needed to make the connection, are broken." Shalom unscrewed the switch plate and pointed out to Mr. Finster the cracked wires that could no longer carry electricity.

"Oh, hi there, Mister! Whatcha doin'?" curious little Naftali asked, as he noticed the man with the fancy tool belt taking apart the light switch.

"Oh, hello there, little fellow! My name is Shalom Lichtman. I'm an electrician. This little old light switch is broken. I need to replace the switch in order for the lights to go back on again."

"Wow!" Naftali exclaimed. "That light switch is so small. The ceiling lamp is so much bigger and it has lots of light bulbs, but it can't work

without that little switch! That little switch probably cost a lot of money because it's so important."

"Actually, it doesn't cost much at all," Shalom replied. "Believe it or not, young man, the light fixture and the bulbs cost quite a lot more than this little switch."

"It doesn't make sense — why should that switch cost so little if the lights can't go on without it? … By the way my name is Naftali, not 'Young Man.'"

"Naftali, let me put it to you this way," Shalom explained in the simplest way possible. "If you have a switch, but no bulbs, the lights won't go on. If you have a switch and you have light bulbs, but no light fixture, the lights won't go on. And guess what? If you have a switch, light bulbs, *and* a light fixture, but no electricity, the lights *still* won't go on."

"I think I'm all confused!" Naftali blurted.

"Naftali, the point is, it is not the cost of a part that determines its importance. It is how the part is used. And in reality, all the parts are equally important, regardless of how much they cost. The lights will go on only if all the parts work together. If one part is broken or missing, the lights will never go on."

"So, that means that to make the lights work, you need to have electricity, a light fixture, light bulbs, *and* a little old switch."

"Now you've got it, Naftali!"

"Thanks, Shalom," a grateful Mr. Finster said. "I couldn't have said it any better myself."

"Tatty, Tatty," Naftali beamed with excitement. "Thanks to Mr. Lichtman, I now understand the mishnah in *Pirkei Avos* you were trying to teach me yesterday!"

"How did he help you?" Mr. Finster asked.

"Mr. Lichtman said that all the parts that make the lights work are important, no matter how much each part costs," Naftali explained. "The Mishnah tells us to be just as careful with a minor mitzvah as with a major one, because we don't know the reward of each mitzvah.* Now I understand what it means. The importance of a mitzvah doesn't go according to what we might think, which is that the more we spend on doing a mitzvah, the more important it is. That's not the way it is.

"The lights can't go on without the cheap switch. That means that since we really don't know the real importance of any mitzvah, we should do every single one that comes our way, and try just as hard to do them all right."

Pirkei Avos 2:1.

A Mouse on the Loose

"Yikes! A mouse!" the girls in Morah Chani's class shrieked.

"Girls, girls, GIRLS! Please quiet down and get into your seats right now!" Morah Chani ordered the children as calmly as she could under the circumstances.

"But, Morah, there's a mouse running loose in the room!" Esti said as she climbed onto her seat.

"EEEEEE! YIKES! LOOK OUT! IT'S COMING THIS WAY! HELP! OUTTA MY WAY!" The girls shrieked even louder than before. Complete pandemonium ruled in Morah Chani's classroom!

"Morah, the mouse jumped out of your candy can when you opened your desk drawer to take a candy out of it!" Hindy said.

"Shaindy, please tell me you didn't," Gitty whispered to her best friend.

"But I did," Shaindy whispered back. "I bought a mouse from the local pet shop and tucked it into a can just like Morah has. Of course, I made a few little holes in the can so it could breathe, and I put in some bread crumbs and a little water in a bottle cap. After school yester-

day, I snuck back into the classroom and switched Morah's candy can for the one that had the mouse inside."

"But didn't I warn you about not doing such *shtick*, even in the month of Adar!" Gitty continued in a disapproving whisper. "I thought I explained pretty clearly why it's wrong to do such things."

"Don't be such a spoilsport," Shaindy whispered her reply. "I made sure no one was around to see me do it, so I won't get caught, unless you snitch. Come on and enjoy the fun. This is just the excitement we need to liven things up around here. I'm having a hard time controlling my own laughter."

Morah Chani called in the principal, who in turn called in Yaakov, the janitor, to catch the mouse.

"Come here, you little mouse! I will catch you yet!" Yaakov shouted as he chased the mouse all around the room.

Naturally, this meant that the girls were almost hysterical as they dodged the mouse on the loose. Books, pencils, and pens — you name it; they were all knocked off the desks. Knapsacks were kicked all over the place. After about fifteen minutes, Yaakov finally caught the mouse and removed it from the classroom. All the girls then went back to their seats, trying to sort out their belongings from amidst the mess.

"Okay," Morah Chani said when the girls had settled down. "Who is responsible for this insensitive prank?"

No one answered. The whole class sat in total silence. Morah Chani walked up and down each row, looking into the faces of each student, trying to find anyone with a guilty expression. Shaindy did not give herself away by showing any guilt on her face. Instead, it was the receipt from the pet store that gave her away. She had forgotten to throw out the receipt after she bought the mouse. Shaindy still had it in her knapsack, and when all the knapsacks were kicked around, the top edge of the receipt had popped out, and the name of the pet shop was clearly visible.

"Well, well, well. What have we here, Shaindy?" Morah Chani said as she pulled the receipt out of Shaindy's knapsack. "So, it appears, Shaindy, that you are the one responsible for all this chaos we just experienced. You do realize that your actions will bring upon you consequences you may not like. I will have no choice but to punish you accordingly. First, while the class will go now to recess, you will stay in the room and clean up this mess that you caused to happen. When the rest of the class returns from recess, this room had better be in proper order.

"Then, during the next recess, you will write a composition describing what you did, why it was wrong to do, and how you intend to make sure nothing like it ever happens again. And of course, the composition will have to be signed by your parents."

"*Oy vei!* I should have listened to my friend, Gitty," Shaindy sighed. "She warned me not to do it. Gitty even reminded me about what Rebbe Yehudah HaNasi taught in *Pirkei Avos*. He said to compare the amount

you spend doing a mitzvah with the reward you will receive for doing it; and compare the amount you gain when doing a sin with the punishment you will receive for doing it."

"Perhaps if Gitty would have reminded you of the last part of the mishnah as well, you would have listened better to her warning," Morah Chani commented.

"What does it say?" Shaindy questioned.

"This is in *Perek Beis*, Mishnah *Aleph*. 'Think of three things and you will not come to sin,'" Morah Chani elaborated. "'Know what is above you — 1) an eye that sees, 2) an ear that hears, and 3) whatever you do is written in a book.'* If you would have thought about how Hashem sees, hears, and records everything you do, I don't think you would have tried such a prank."

During the recesses that followed, Shaindy cleaned up the classroom and completed her written assignment. And from that day on, Shaindy still kept her sense of humor, but no longer practiced insensitive pranks.

Pirkei Avos 2:1.

New Tefillin

"**I**'m sorry, but this pair of tefillin cannot be salvaged," the *sofer*, Rabbi Scribner, sadly reported. "The *retzuos* are mangled, the *battim* that house the *parashios* are so warped out of shape that they are beyond repair, and the *parashios* themselves — oy, I've never come across such a *possel* set of *parashios* since Hurricane Katrina! What did you do; did you put these tefillin in a washing machine or something?"

"Well, um … er, yes; sort of," Reuven Wellerberg stammered under his breath.

"WHAT?!" Rabbi Scribner exclaimed in disbelief.

"Well, um … er, you see — *oy*, this is so embarrassing," Reuven tried to muster up the courage to tell what had really happened. "I was walking slowly on my way home from shul this morning, along the edge of the sidewalk near the curb, lost deep in thought. I work as a handyman and business is not so good lately …."

"Eh, maybe you can get straight to the point. I still have other work to do," Rabbi Scribner politely suggested. "If you don't mind, please, just tell me only what happened to the tefillin."

"Oh, yeah. I was getting to that," Reuven said as he collected his thoughts. "Since I was lost in thought, thinking about when will be the next time I get called upon to do a job, I didn't see the speeding car cutting around a slower-moving car. It rained last night and puddles were still on the streets. Suddenly, I was snapped out of my daydreaming by a big '*SPLAT*'! I was *shpritzed* all over with muddy water. I went home to change into dry clothing, and that's when it happened."

"When what happened?" Rabbi Scribner asked as he tried not to lose his patience while waiting for Reuven Wellerberg to finish his story.

"My wife decided it was best to wash my muddy clothes right away, while there was still a chance that the mud stains could be washed out," Reuven continued his story. "My three-year-old noticed my tallis and tefillin spread out over the dining room table to dry out. He innocently thought that my wife had forgotten to put those items into the washing machine along with the other clothes. When no one was looking, he climbed up on a chair and added the tallis and tefillin into the washing machine. By the time we figured out where the tallis and tefillin had disappeared to — it was too late! We managed to save the tallis, but the tefillin …."

"Ah hah! So now I understand everything," Rabbi Scribner said as he stroked his beard. "You do realize you will have to purchase a new pair of tefillin. Since business is a bit slow for you, I will show you a few pairs of tefillin that you can look at that are within a low price range."

"Absolutely not!" Reuven declared. "If I needed to buy a circular saw, I'm sure I wouldn't look at the price tag. I would probably spend whatever it cost to get the best one out there to do the job I need it for. So, too, I'm sure that Hashem would want me to spend whatever amount it would cost to buy the best pair of tefillin available to fulfill the mitzvah of putting on tefillin."

Reuven Wellerberg chose a nice pair of tefillin of the highest quality. He spent $980 for it — and that included a new tefillin bag. Before going to pick up the new tefillin, Reuven explained to his wife that he felt that he was doing the right thing by spending so much on an important mitzvah. He assured her that Hashem would help them financially and that He would not let them down.

"R-R-R-RING!" Reuven's telephone rang the moment he walked in the door after returning home with his brand-new tefillin.

"Hello, Mr. Wellerberg. This is Mr. Gordon," the voice on the phone said. "The handyman I was using to finish my basement caught the flu. There is a little bit more work that must be completed before Shabbos, because my son and daughter-in-law are coming in from Israel to stay with us for a while. My handyman told me to hire someone else to take over the job and that I should pay the balance I owe him to the new handyman. The balance is $980. Do you want to do the job?"

Reuven paused a moment to contemplate the situation. "I can't believe this is happening," he thought. "$980! Rabban Gamliel taught. 'Make [Hashem's] will like your will, so that He shall make your will like His'* — meaning, spend money to do a mitzvah the same way you would spend for yourself; and Hashem will make your needs His needs." Then Reuven answered Mr. Gordon, "Of course I'll take the job! Just give me your address and I'll be there first thing in the morning after *Shacharis* and a little bit of breakfast."

* *Pirkei Avos* 2:4.

A Night To Remember

"Hey, Avi, are you gonna join us at Zevi's house this coming Sunday night?" Binny asked.

"Why, what's the occasion?" Avi answered with a question.

"It's Super Bowl Sunday!" Binny announced. "A bunch of us are gonna be gathering around Zevi's new surround-sound radio system to listen to the game live. Zevi will be serving pizza, popcorn, and soda. Why don't you come and join us? You'll have lots of fun!"

"Binny, we can't do that," Avi stated firmly. "We have a *seder* to learn

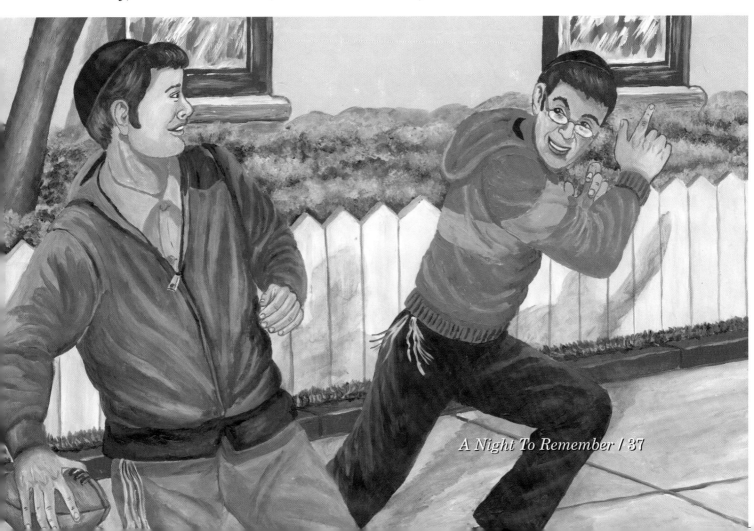

Gemara every Sunday night after *Maariv*. We'll just have to listen to the score later on the radio."

"Avi, don't you realize you'll be missing the game of a lifetime?" Binny asked, dismayed at the thought of Avi not wanting to join him at Zevi's house. "We can make up the time. We will learn twice as long next Sunday. How about it?"

"NO WAY!" Avi insisted. "I love sports as much as you do; however, they don't run my life. I don't know about you, but I draw the line when sports get in the way of my learning. I can't stop you if you want to go to Zevi's house. You know where to find me Sunday night after *Maariv* if you decide to change your mind."

That Sunday night, Super Bowl Sunday, Avi could be found in the shul by himself, reviewing the *Gemara* he had learned in yeshivah. He got so carried away with his learning that he lost track of the time. Before Avi

knew it, it was eleven o'clock. He thought about how worried his parents might be, wondering where he was so late at night. Avi grabbed his coat and headed on home.

The walk home was usually very safe, so Avi was surprised when he saw a gang of teenage hooligans wandering the streets, looking to make some trouble. They spotted Avi walking alone and began to follow him. Avi was frightened by the thought that he might be attacked. There was no place to run or hide. The gang was fast approaching, and they surrounded him from all sides. Avi started to say the *Tehillim* that he knew by heart. As he felt his heart begin pounding like a runaway locomotive, Avi began to beg for Hashem's help, using whatever words of his own he could muster.

"Hey, Jew-boy!" the gang leader called out as they closed in on Avi. "Do ya got any money?"

"Er … uh … no," Avi answered, terrified. "P-p-please m-m-move out of the way s-s-s-so I c-c-can p-p-pass."

"HA, HA, HA!" the gang leader laughed loudly as he pulled out a knife to scare Avi. "We ain't movin' till we get some money!" The other gang members began waving baseball bats and heavy metal chains threateningly. "You *are* gonna give us your money or we're gonna beat the living daylights out of ya!"

Suddenly, the gang members heard a booming voice call, "Hey, you little hoodlums, if you lay one finger on that kid, I'll make mincemeat out of all of you!"

The gang members all turned to see where the voice was coming from. They were amazed to see a tall man wearing a heavy overcoat and a black hat. He was bearing down on them like a steamroller, *tzitzis* flying and fists raised.

"Yikes! That guy must be at least seven feet tall!"

"Yeah, man. He looks like he must weigh in at 360 pounds!"

"Hey, guys, he's all muscle! He's built like a brick wall!"

"I SAY LET'S GET OUTTA HERE BEFORE HE PULVERIZES US!" And with that last comment, the gang of hoodlums left Avi alone and ran for *their* lives!

"Thank you! Thank you, mister! You saved my life!" Avi expressed himself with great relief. "Hashem answered my *tefillos*. He sent you as his messenger to save me. That's the only possible explanation!"

The man smiled gently at Avi. "For Hashem to cause me to pop up here in the nick of time to save you, you must have had some special *zechus*. Please tell me, what did you do that was so special?"

"I didn't do anything special," Avi replied, puzzled. "I just did what I always do on Sundays after yeshivah. Every Sunday night, lots of guys from my class voluntarily come to learn and review *Gemara* in our local shul. Tonight, since it's Super Bowl Sunday, I seem to have been the only one from my class that showed up in shul to learn. I lost track of time and ended up being out so late at night alone. I don't recall doing anything so special."

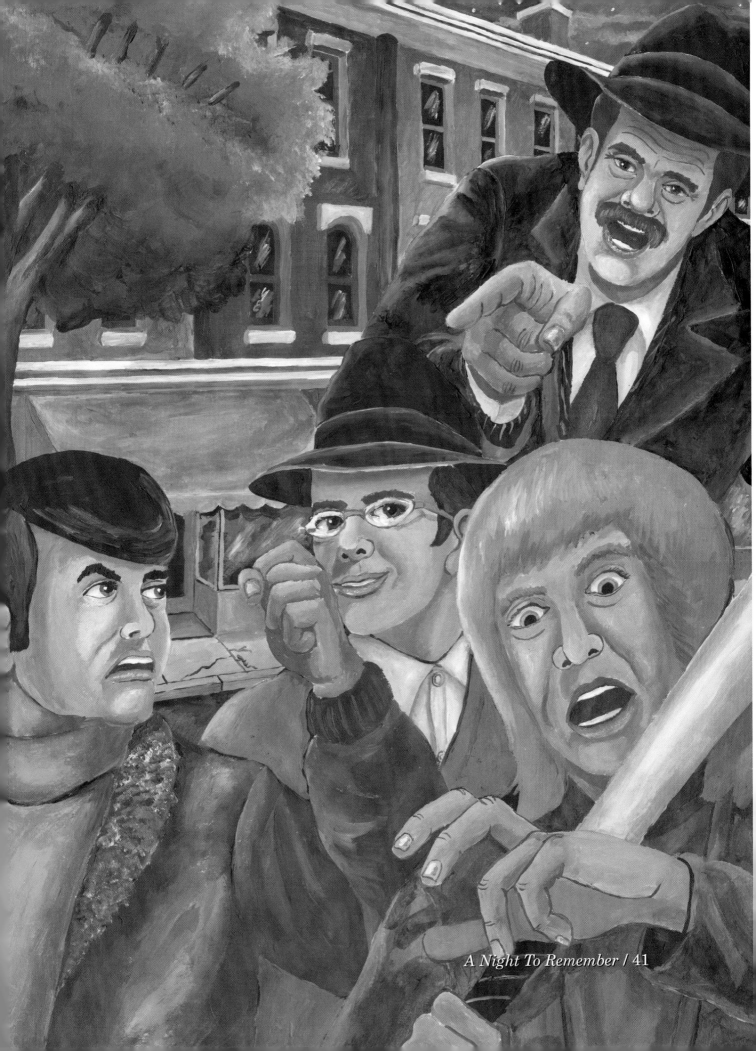

"You overcame your desire to listen to the Super Bowl live and kept your weekly learning *seder* instead — I'd say that's something special! You were saved tonight because you followed what Rabban Gamliel teaches in *Pirkei Avos*, 'Nullify your will before [Hashem's] will, so that He will nullify the will of others before your will.'*

"You nullified your desire to listen to the Super Bowl to do Hashem's will — to learn His Torah. Hashem nullified that gang's desire to beat and rob you by sending me to your rescue, as you requested His help."

Avi thanked the man once again and then went straight home without any further incident. He told his parents about everything that had transpired that night. Avi never again met the strange man who had suddenly popped up out of nowhere and come to his rescue. One thing that Avi did know — Hashem was definitely watching over him with special care on that Sunday night — a night to remember always.

Pirkei Avos 2:4.

Zutchka

"**Z**utchka, is it true that you took a pair of boots from Yankel's shoe store without paying for them?" Rabbi Zeesha Herschel asked.

"I sure did!" boasted Zutchka. "I needed them, so I took them!"

"And the bloody nose?" Rabbi Zeesha Herschel continued questioning the Jewish peasant.

"Oh, that little thing happened when Yankel tried to stop me from taking the boots," Zutchka said without any feelings of regret. "It's his own fault. I said I would eventually pay for the boots. Yankel stood in the doorway and tried to stop me, so I just shoved him out of the way. BOOM! He went *smack* right into the wall and that's how he got a bloody nose."

"Zutchka, you can't go on like this!" Rabbi Zeesha Herschel declared. "You just can't go barging into stores and taking whatever you want by force. You may be telling all the shopkeepers that you will pay them one day, but we all know that hasn't happened yet, even though it's been years! Zutchka, you used to be so good when you were a little boy. What happened to you?"

"I grew up. That's what happened," Zutchka answered. "I grew big and strong. I began to realize that there was no one in the whole shtetl as big and as strong as I am. I figured I should take advantage of my gifts. I take whatever I want, whenever I want, and no one can stop me. Everyone around here knows they'd better show me respect, or else they'll face some music they don't like if you know what I mean." Zutchka grinned fiercely and showed Rabbi Zeesha Herschel his two strong fists.

"Zutchka, you've gone way too far," Rabbi Zeesha Herschel chided. "The villagers have had enough of your antics. They requested that I ban you from the village. If you don't repent and change your ways, I'm afraid you will leave me no choice. I will have to fulfill the villagers' request, and you'll be forced to leave the shtetl."

"Ha! You don't scare me, Rabbi," Zutchka stated defiantly. "There's nobody here in this entire village that has the courage or strength to force me to leave — not even *you,* Rabbi!"

"Zutchka, just look at this apple," Rabbi Zeesha Herschel said, taking an apple from the bowl on the table. "Did you know that you two share things in common? The apple grew from a tiny seed; you grew from a tiny cell. The apple is now in full ripeness; you are now in the prime of your strength. Uneaten, the apple will eventually wither and

rot, just as you will eventually grow old and feeble. When your time comes to die you will be buried in the same earth in which everyone else is buried. All your feats of strength, your showing off, and all the illegally obtained riches you have accumulated will be useless. However, your *neshamah* will stand before Hashem and you will have to give an accounting of all your actions. Hashem will reward you for any good deeds that you have done in your lifetime. And by the same token, you can rest assured that He will certainly punish you for all the bad deeds that you have done …. Do you think that you are tougher than Hashem, eh, Zutchka?"

"Oh, no!" Zutchka gasped. "I never thought of those things before. Rabbi Zeesha Herschel, please forgive me for acting with chutzpah toward you. Please, teach me how I can change my ways. I have been acting this way for so long that I don't think it's possible."

"Of course it's possible, Zutchka! You just need to put your mind to it," Rabbi Zeesha Herschel reassured him. "Just keep thinking about what Akavia Ben Mehalalel taught. 'From where did you come? You came from a tiny cell that could have easily spoiled. Where are you going? You will end up going to a place of dust, worms, and maggots. And before whom you are destined to give an accounting and a reckoning? The King of all kings, The Holy One, Blessed is He.'*

"Zutchka, if you will always keep these thoughts in your mind you will never ever dream of having *gaavah* — seeking too much honor and glory; *taavoh* — having a never-satisfied appetite for the best of everything at all costs, even if it means stealing to get it; and believing in your own greatness. If you will work on eradicating these, you will not come to sin."

"Thank you, Rabbi. I will work on doing all that you suggest and with Hashem's help, I hope to become a better person," Zutchka humbly replied.

Pirkei Avos 3:1.

The Parking Space

"Look! There's a parking space, Tatty," Hindy said as she pointed to an open space between the parked cars on the busy avenue.

Mr. Klieger immediately started to back into the space before anyone else would take it. Suddenly, without warning, another car zoomed up behind them, seemingly out of nowhere. The other driver speeded up and maneuvered his car, front end first, behind the Klieger's car, in an effort to "steal" the parking space.

Mr. Klieger honked his horn to get the other driver's attention. He then motioned, as politely as he could, that he had seen the spot first.

The other driver honked back annoyingly. He opened his window and began shouting insults at Mr. Klieger, "You know you've got some nerve, mister! I'm in the middle of pulling into this parking space; and *you* come on right along and try to steal this spot from right under my nose! Get lost!"

"WHAT?!" Hindy protested in amazement. "You were here first, Tatty! That man is lying through his teeth. He's definitely not a nice person!"

"That's enough, Hindy," Mr. Klieger said. "No need to get upset over a silly old parking space. Please quiet down and let me handle it."

Mr. Klieger turned to the other driver, "Excuse me, sir. I don't mean you any disrespect, but I'm sure you saw me backing into this parking space before you got here. I'm sure that you want to do the right thing and allow me to finish parking. I do wish you luck, though, in finding another space."

The other driver did not take kindly to Mr. Klieger's kind words. He stormed out of his car, his temper flaring. He waved his fists threateningly as he approached.

"ARE YOU CALLING ME A LIAR?" he shouted at the top of his lungs. "IT'S *ME* WHO GOT HERE FIRST, NOT *YOU*! Now are you going to move out of the way, or do you want to make something of this?"

"Um …. no, sir," Mr. Klieger responded in a surprisingly calm manner, as he began to pull out. "If you want this parking space so badly, you can have it. To me, it's not worth fighting over. Take it and enjoy it. Have a nice day."

"Tatty, why didn't you stand up for your rights?" Hindy complained as they drove off. "That man was clearly wrong! There was no need to be afraid of him. He might have been a little bit taller than you, Tatty, but if he started to fight you, you would have won. You're much stronger than that guy will ever be."

"You're right, Hindy," Mr. Klieger replied. "I *am* much stronger than that man. I conquered my *Yetzer Hora*, and he didn't.

"Ben Zoma says in *Pirkei Avos*, 'Who is strong? The one who subdues his inclination.'* Ben Zoma quotes the *pasuk* in *Mishlei*, 'Better is he who is slow to anger than a strong man; and one who rules his spirit [desires] is better than a conqueror of a city.'"**

Hindy took her father's words to heart. "On second thought, Tatty," she said, "I'm glad you controlled your temper. If you would have gotten into a fight with that nasty person, the commotion would have brought the police, and then ...."

"Those were precisely my thoughts, Hindy," Mr. Klieger interjected. "Because we controlled ourselves, we avoided other problems that could have escalated from that incident. I'm sure that because we did the right thing, we will find another parking space and still have plenty of time to shop."

Pirkei Avos 4:1.

**Mishlei* 16:32.

Who Is Truly Rich

"**O**y, Mendy, I feel so bad for you," Herschel moaned as he spoke to his old school friend. "When I came to visit the old home town, I heard about you. I'm so sorry to hear that you didn't make it big. How happy can you be as only the owner of one small, measly shoe store?"

"Very happy," Mendy answered. "Hashem blessed me with a wonderful wife and four fabulous children — two boys and two girls. I make a decent living from my shoe store. My family and I live in a small, but comfortable, home that I own ....”

“Ah! You call *that* living happily?” Herschel questioned with a sneer. “Take a good look at *me*. Do you see the fancy suit I’m wearing? I made it to the big time and have become quite wealthy. You should learn from me how to live happily. I own businesses and real estate in California and in Florida. And now I’m here in New York looking to expand my investments.

“Back in California, I own a mansion with 27 bedrooms, 15 bathrooms, an Olympic-size swimming pool, and a six-car garage that houses four Mercedes Benzes along with two limousines. I can afford to buy my wife and five children the best of everything that there is out there to buy .... Oh, by the way, did I mention anything yet about my mansion in Florida?”

“No, but that won’t be necessary,” Mendy replied. “I’ve heard enough to realize that you are not really rich or happy at all.”

“What? How can you say that after all the things I just described?” Herschel questioned, baffled.

“Herschel, please don’t get insulted by what I’m about to say,” Mendy began to explain. “Can you please tell me why you need so many cars and such huge mansions with so many rooms just to house so few people? You probably had to hire many, many workers to care for your mansions; and let us not forget the expense of having the best alarms and security systems available to prevent thefts. I’ll bet you probably tremble every time someone comes too close to any of your cars, because you’re afraid they may get scratched or damaged by accident. And your suit — my, how carefully you must have to eat while wearing it!

“I can’t imagine how you can find some quality family time with your busy schedule. Do you manage to daven all three *tefillos* with a minyan every day? Do you have a set time when you learn Torah, or do you even take the opportunity to learn Torah at all? I’d guess that you probably don’t give as much to *tzedakah* as you should, since you spend so much money living such a materialistic lifestyle. Herschel, *I’m* the one who is truly rich — *not you!*”

"How can that possibly be true?" a bewildered Herschel questioned.

"It seems to me that you've forgotten some of the things you learned in yeshivah way back in the good old days," Mendy pointed out. "Don't you remember learning about what Ben Zoma taught in *Pirkei Avos*? 'Who is truly rich? He who is happy with his portion.'* *Baruch Hashem*, I am happy and content with what I have. I am able to support my family because I work hard. I don't have any desire to have more than what I need. As a result, I don't live in constant fear of being robbed, nor do I tremble in anguish over every scratch my car gets. On Shabbos, I eat without worrying what will happen if I get a *cholent* stain on my suit. My family and I get to spend lots of quality family time together. I always daven with a minyan three times every day. I manage to find time to learn with and help my children with their homework whenever they need it. Every week I attend the Rav's Torah discourse. At least three times a week — and sometimes more — I learn with a good friend of mine ...."

"Okay, okay, I see the picture you are trying to paint," a disgruntled Herschel interrupted. "What you are basically saying is, a religious Jew should not try to become rich."

Pirkei Avos 4:1.

"Oh, no! Heaven forbid! Please don't get me wrong," Mendy reassured Herschel. "On the contrary, there is nothing wrong with becoming rich, as long as you continue to live in a Torah lifestyle. Rich people are entitled to live a comfortable lifestyle within their means. They just need to remember why Hashem allowed them to enjoy a rich portion. They should not get carried away by the demands of the materialistic world. After all, if Hashem would not make people rich, then who would be the supporters of Torah institutions and the poor?"

Herschel took his friend Mendy's lesson to heart. It was not an easy thing to do, but nonetheless, Herschel worked hard at it and eventually, over a period of time, he became a changed person. Oh, don't worry about him! Although Herschel cut back on his lifestyle, he still remains quite wealthy today — only now he has his priorities straight.

What's the Big Deal?

"Berel, the more I think about the Rabbi's sermon on Shabbos, the more it doesn't make any sense," Shimon Gold, the proprietor of Gold's Antique Shop, sighed.

"What did he say that you don't understand?" Berel asked.

"The Rabbi said that Hashem created the world with great love and

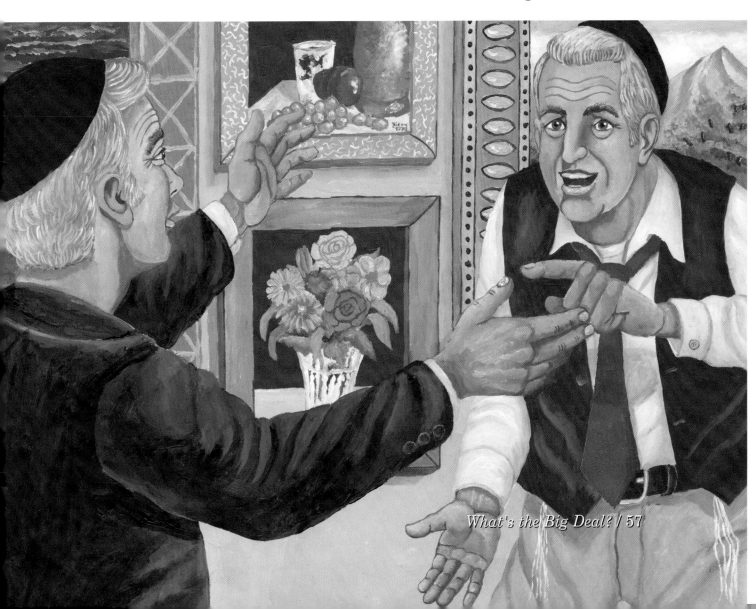

devotion to every detail. All the completed parts work together like a well-oiled machine. If even one pin or gear were to be removed, the whole machine would either stop or malfunction. The same holds true with the wicked. When they sin, they are punished as though they destroyed a whole world," Shimon Gold repeated verbatim a detail of the Rabbi's sermon. "It doesn't make any sense to me. What's the big deal — if a pin or gear is removed, just replace the pin or gear! If the wicked sin, let them be punished for that part of creation that they ruined — not for destroying a whole world!"

"Excuse me! Coming through! Watch out, please," Duvi interrupted Berel and Shimon's conversation as he entered the store with a delivery of numerous packages.

"Duvi, watch where you're going!" Shimon Gold warned. "Why must you carry in all the packages all at once? Why don't you bring them from your truck in two trips? Right now you have the packages piled so high; I don't know how you can see in front of yourself. You know those packages have delicate items inside. You should be more careful, Duvi."

"Don't worry about a thing, Mr. Gold," Duvi reassured. "I have everything under control. I do things like this every day. It saves me lots of time. Now just tell me where you want me to put all this stuff."

"Put the packages down there, in the empty space I prepared for them, over to your right," Mr. Gold said, indicating a cleared area on the floor.

Duvi started to walk toward the right, completely unaware that one of his shoelaces had become untied. His feet became entangled in the laces as he walked. Losing his balance, Duvi began to topple forward.

"Watch out! You're falling! Don't you dare drop *anything*!" Mr. Gold shouted as he shuddered at the thought of what was about to happen.

"Don't you worry, Mr. Gold. I've … I've got … got everything under con … con … controoooooooooOOOL!" Duvi cried out as his juggling act came to an end and he fell to the floor, with the packages crashing down all around him.

Berel rushed over to check that Duvi was okay. Shimon hurried to open up the packages to make sure that no merchandise had been damaged in the fall. Everything was fine except for one item.

"*Oy, vei!*" Shimon cried out in despair. "What am I going to do? Look at this painting. The lower edge of the painting has a big hole in it! It's completely ruined!"

"Ah, what's the big deal?" Berel teased. "The hole is only in a very small part of the painting. Just put on a little patch and PRESTO! You're back in business and you can sell the painting again — it'll be just like brand-new!"

"What?! I can't do that!" Shimon exclaimed. "Who is going to buy a painting with a patch on it? If someone does choose to buy the painting, I could never sell it for its full price. The damage has greatly decreased the whole painting's overall value."

"Well, now, Shimon, perhaps from what just happened here you can better understand the Rabbi's explanation of the mishnah," Berel suggested. "It states that the world was created with ten sayings instead of just one saying, to teach us that Hashem punishes the wicked who destroyed a world that was created with ten sayings, and rewards the righteous who sustain the world that was created in ten sayings.* The Rabbi's parable about the well-oiled machine is no different from what happened with your expensive painting.

Pirkei Avos 5:1.

"Look how upset you became when you realized that even though only a small area of the painting became damaged, you still will never be able to sell it for its previous full value. Patch or no patch, the bottom line is that the damage has permanently decreased the painting's whole value — not just that of a small part."

"You are so right, Berel," Shimon conceded. "I guess this incident clearly happened to help me to better understand the Rabbi's sermon."

Glossary

Baruch Hashem – Blessed is Hashem; Thank Hashem

battim – tefillin boxes containing verses of prayers

chutzpah – impudence

daven – to pray

gaavah – pride

Gemara – the Talmud

Maariv – the evening prayers

minyan – a quorum of 10 men

mishnah – a segment of *Pirkei Avos*

Mishlei – *Proverbs*

neshamah – a soul

parashios – scrolls

pasuk – a verse

perek – a chapter

Pirkei Avos – *Ethics of the Fathers*

possel – invalid; not usable

Rav – a rabbi; a spiritual leader

retzuos – the leather straps of tefillin

seder – a set time, usually for learning

Shacharis – the morning prayers

shpritzed – splashed

shtetl – a village

shtick – here, mischievous actions

shul – a synagogue

sofer – a religious scribe

taavoh – desire

tallis – a prayer shawl

tefillin – phylacteries

tefillos – prayers

Tehillim – *Psalms*

tzedakah – charity

tzitzis – a fringed garment

Yetzer Hora – the evil inclination

zechus – merit

This volume is part of
THE ARTSCROLL SERIES®
an ongoing project of
translations, commentaries and expositions
on Scripture, Mishnah, Talmud, Halachah,
liturgy, history, the classic Rabbinic writings,
biographies and thought.

For a brochure of current publications
visit your local Hebrew bookseller
or contact the publisher:

Mesorah Publications, ltd

4401 Second Avenue
Brooklyn, New York 11232
(718) 921-9000
www.artscroll.com